Dear Parents and Educators,

Welcome to Penguin Young Readers! As parents and educators, you know that each child develops at his or her own pace—in terms of speech, critical thinking, and, of course, reading. Penguin Young Readers recognizes this fact. As a result, each Penguin Young Readers book is assigned a traditional easy-to-read level (1–4) as well as a Guided Reading Level (A–P). Both of these systems will help you choose the right book for your child. Please refer to the back of each book for specific leveling information. Penguin Young Readers features esteemed authors and illustrators, stories about favorite characters, fascinating nonfiction, and more!

Zoobles!™: Birthday Surprise

LEVEL 2

GUIDED READING LEVEL **H**

This book is perfect for a **Progressing Reader** who:
- can figure out unknown words by using picture and context clues;
- can recognize beginning, middle, and ending sounds;
- can make and confirm predictions about what will happen in the text; and
- can distinguish between fiction and nonfiction.

Here are some **activities** you can do during and after reading this book:
- Sight Words: Sight words are frequently used words that readers must know just by looking at them. They are known instantly, on sight. Knowing these words helps children develop into efficient readers. As you read the story, point out the sight words below.

about	do	him	their	they
be	going	now	then	where

- Make Connections: Watson had a wonderful time playing games and eating cake at his surprise birthday party. Can you think of your favorite birthday? What made it so special?

Remember, sharing the love of reading with a child is the best gift you can give!

—Bonnie Bader, EdM
  Penguin Young Readers program

D1053403

*Penguin Young Readers are leveled by independent reviewers applying the standards developed by Irene Fountas and Gay Su Pinnell in *Matching Books to Readers: Using Leveled Books in Guided Reading*, Heinemann, 1999.

Penguin Young Readers
Published by the Penguin Group
Penguin Group (USA) Inc., 375 Hudson Street, New York, New York 10014, USA
Penguin Group (Canada), 90 Eglinton Avenue East, Suite 700, Toronto, Ontario M4P 2Y3, Canada
(a division of Pearson Penguin Canada Inc.)
Penguin Books Ltd., 80 Strand, London WC2R 0RL, England
Penguin Group Ireland, 25 St. Stephen's Green, Dublin 2, Ireland
(a division of Penguin Books Ltd.)
Penguin Group (Australia), 250 Camberwell Road, Camberwell, Victoria 3124, Australia
(a division of Pearson Australia Group Pty. Ltd.)
Penguin Books India Pvt. Ltd., 11 Community Centre, Panchsheel Park, New Delhi—110 017, India
Penguin Group (NZ), 67 Apollo Drive, Rosedale, Auckland 0632, New Zealand
(a division of Pearson New Zealand Ltd.)
Penguin Books (South Africa) (Pty.) Ltd., 24 Sturdee Avenue,
Rosebank, Johannesburg 2196, South Africa

Penguin Books Ltd., Registered Offices: 80 Strand, London WC2R 0RL, England

The publisher does not have any control over and does not assume any responsibility for author or third-party websites or their content.

Zoobles™ and © 2012 Spin Master Ltd. Published by Penguin Young Readers, an imprint of Penguin Group (USA) Inc., 345 Hudson Street, New York, New York 10014. Manufactured in China.

ISBN 978-0-448-46166-3   10 9 8 7 6 5 4 3 2 1

PENGUIN YOUNG READERS

LEVEL
PROGRESSING
READER
2

Zoobles! BIRTHDAY SURPRISE

by Lana Edelman
pencils by MadPark Digital Inc.
color by Artful Doodlers Ltd.

Penguin Young Readers
An Imprint of Penguin Group (USA) Inc.

Today is a special day.

Today is Watson

the Moose's birthday!

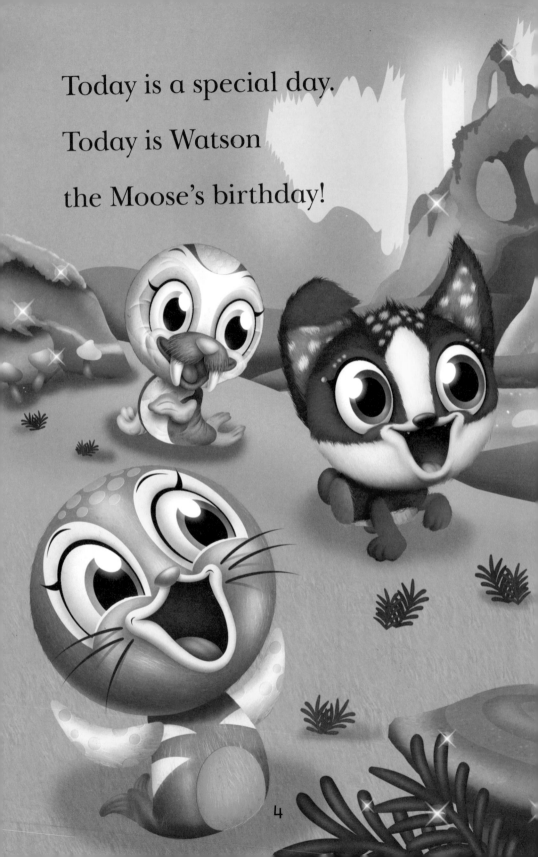

Watson's friends will do

something special for him.

They will throw him

a surprise birthday party!

Watson's friends talk
about their plans.

Cesealia the Sea Lion
and Tuskee the Walrus
will prepare for the party.
Doxy the Dog will
play with Watson
to keep him busy.

Cesealia and Tuskee practice
popping open on their Happitats.

They shout, "Surprise!"

Then they decorate for the party.

Watson is going

to be so surprised!

Meanwhile, Doxy and Watson

play hide-and-seek.

First, Doxy looks for Watson.

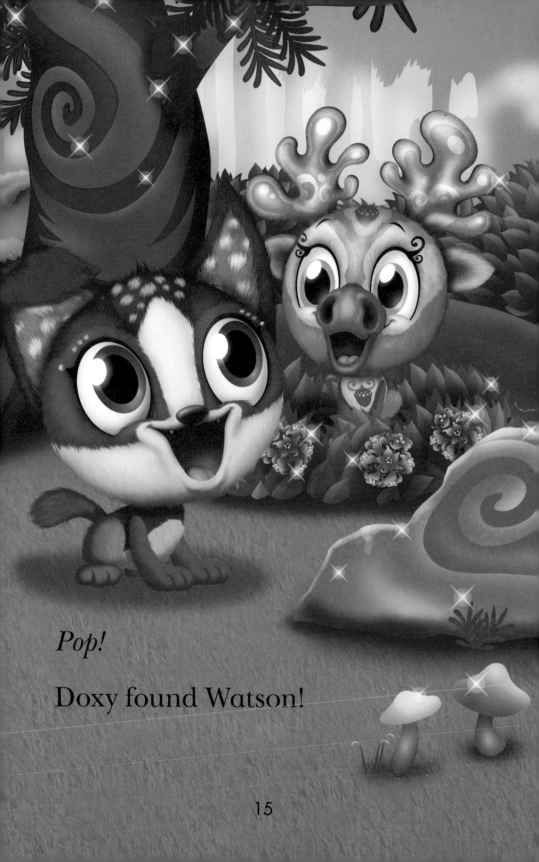

Pop!

Doxy found Watson!

Now it is Watson's turn

to look for Doxy.

But where is Watson?

Is he lost?

Suddenly, Doxy, Cesealia,
and Tuskee pop open
and shout, "Surprise!"

Watson is very surprised!

He did not know that his friends

were planning a party for him.

They are so clever!

Now it is time for games.

Who will get the candy

to fall out?

Watson wins!

He gets lots of treats.

Hooray!

He shares the candy

with his friends.

Now the Zoobles play

Duck, Duck, Goose.

Watson is the goose.

Who will get tapped next?

Watson taps Cesealia.

But she rolls out of the circle!

Where is she going?

Cesealia goes to get the cake!

Watson blows out his candles

and makes a wish.

Then he eats cake

with his friends.

Watson had a great
surprise birthday party.
He has such wonderful friends!